For Tallulah
—C.D.

The McClure Twins: Make It Fashion
Text copyright © 2021 by Ava McClure and Alexis McClure
Cowritten by Sundee Frazier
Illustrations copyright © 2021 by Courtney Dawson

ISBN 978-0-06-302952-1

The artist used Procreate and Photoshop to create
the digital illustrations for this book.
Typography by Rachel Zegar
21 22 23 24 25   PC   10 9 8 7 6 5 4 3 2 1
❖
First Edition

★The McClure Twins★
Make It Fashion

written by Ava and Alexis McClure

illustrated by Courtney Dawson

HARPER

An Imprint of HarperCollinsPublishers

Ava and

Alexis are sisters.

And when they were just itty-bitty, they discovered something really big . . .

Yep, Ava and Alexis discovered they were
more than just sisters. They were twins . . .

identical

twins.

This means there's a lot about them that's the same.

Same room,

same friends,

same way to eat their same
favorite snacks.

They have a few toys that
are different, but the *same*
brother gets into them all.

Sameness is their thing.

At least that's what Alexis and Ava thought as they started planning their very first . . .

TWINTASTIC F

ASHION SHOW!

(It's sort of a big deal.)

They agreed on the theme,

the guest list,

and the music.

There was only one thing they didn't see quite
the same: their outfits for the show.

Ava, who loves everything fancy, pulled out sparkly gemstones and poofy skirts, while Alexis skimmed her closet for the perfect pants and sneakers. She likes to keep it old-school cool.

"We should wear this for the fashion show!" both sisters said, holding up their different outfit choices.

"We're twins, Sissy. We have to match," said Ava.

"You're being Bossy McBossy Pants," teased Alexis.

"I am not. I am being the oldest. And younger sisters listen to the oldest!"

"The oldest?!"

"Yes, the oldest. I'm exactly one minute older according to my precise calculations."

Pfft.

Alexis didn't want to wear fancy outfits almost as much as she didn't want to be a minute younger.

Alexis and Ava started to worry. They thought twins had to like all the same things. Could twins be different from one another? Was it possible for twins to be . . . *mismatched*?!

One thing Ava and Alexis did know was that they liked doing everything side by side. No matter what, they promised to

strut together and
make it fashion.

PINKY
PROMISE.

That meant working as a team even if they didn't agree at first.

Since there was still a show to put on, the twins decided to set the stage.

Alexis drew pictures for the backdrop.

Ava used her eye for pizzazz to create the runway.

It takes two to rip the runway

Both sisters reserved seats for the special guests.

Mr. Poofy can sit right up front.

Ava and Alexis were having so much fun, they *almost* forgot about being different.

When there was nothing left to do but choose their outfits, the sisters thought of an amazing idea.

They gave each other a fist bump and headed to their closets.

"It's showtime!"

The curtains opened. Ava and Alexis sashayed down
the runway. The crowd went wild.

They mixed and matched poofy skirts with parachute pants, bedazzled sparkly gemstones on hoodies, and decorated baseball caps with flowers and bows.

To top it off, they wore glittery high-top sneakers.

The twins mixed a little bit of Ava and matched a little bit of
Alexis, creating a whole new mismatched, fancy, old-school style.
It was fabulously twintastic!

Ava and Alexis discovered twins can be the same and different.
Twins can mix and match.

It takes two to rip the runway

At the end of the runway, they hooked fingers
and repeated their twinship pinky promise:
**"Strut together and
make it fashion!"**

akes _two_ to

Mama and Dada were so proud. "Being the same makes you two special, but being different makes you . . . you!"

After they hugged, there was only one thing left to do . . .

"Dance it out!

Dance it out!"
Twin style.

★The McClure Twins' Fierce Fashion Tips★

We love making everything fashion! You can, too, by following these five fabulous tips.

Tip #1:
The best accessory is a smile.

Tip #2:
No matter what, always make it your own.

Tip #3:
Two words: #BIGHAIR, #DON'TCARE.
(Okay, that's four words!)

★ **Tip #4:**

Be kind.
Be confident.
Be cool.

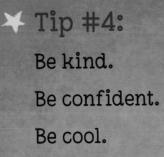

"Get it, Jersey!"

★ **Tip #5:**

Wear lots and lots of colors. And when in doubt, add a dash of sparkles.

Bonus Tip:

Whatever you do, strut together and make it fashion!